THOMAS & FRIENDS

The Tall Friend

A new Safari Park was opening and all the engines had important jobs to do.

Percy and Edward's trucks were **full** of food for the animals.

"I'm taking the **tallest** animal to the park," puffed Thomas, excitedly.

The other engines tried to guess what it could be.

It was a **giraffe!**

All the engines wheeshed with wonder.

Thomas couldn't wait to show the children the **tallest** animal on Sodor!

"You must wait for the giraffe keeper," said Cranky. But Thomas was in too much of a rush and he puffed away.

Thomas **puffed** happily along with the giraffe, but it wasn't long before they came to a low bridge.

"Sit down, Mr Giraffe," Thomas chuffed.

But the giraffe didn't want to sit down, so they couldn't fit under the bridge!

Thomas heard a whistle.
It was Gordon.

"Out of the way," Gordon tooted,
crossly. "You must get the keeper.
The giraffe will do what he tells him."

"No, I can manage," puffed Thomas,
and he reversed into a siding.

Then, Edward **chuffed** up with his trucks full of rosy, red apples. The apples gave Thomas an idea.

Perhaps the giraffe would get sleepy and sit down if he ate some apples?

The giraffe liked Edward's apples. He **ate**, and **ate**, and **ate** … but he didn't sit down.

Edward was upset that all his apples had been eaten.

"You **must** go back and get the keeper, Thomas," Edward puffed, crossly.

Thomas was worried. The Fat Controller was waiting for him and he still couldn't get under the bridge.

Just then, Percy **puffed** along with a truck full of leaves.

Thomas thought the giraffe might sit down if he ate some of the leaves.

The giraffe loved the leaves! He **munched** and **munched** until there were none left.

And then, finally, he sat down and closed his eyes.

"He's asleep!" peeped Thomas. "At last, we can go under the bridge to the Safari Park!"

Thomas **clickety-clacked** along the track and under the bridge all the way to the Safari Park.

The Fat Controller was there and he was **cross**. There were **no** apples and **no** leaves for the animals to eat and the tallest animal was fast asleep!

"I'm sorry, Sir," wheeshed Thomas. "I should have waited for the keeper."

Thomas **puffed** his fastest to fetch the keeper and take him to the park, and then he **chuffed** away to get more apples and more leaves.

When Thomas finally puffed back into the Safari Park, the giraffe was wide awake!

He heard Thomas **toot** and stretched out his **long** neck to his new friend.

"Welcome to Sodor, Mr Giraffe!" peeped Thomas, happily. "It's a wonderful place to live!"

PEEP! PEEP!

The End